To Malcolm
—C.N.

To Amelia
—A.A.

Text copyright © 1994 by Caroline Ness
Illustrations copyright © 1994 by Alex Ayliffe
Produced by Mathew Price Ltd.
First American Edition, 1995
Printed in Hong Kong. All rights reserved.

Let's Get a Puppy

By Caroline Ness
Illustrated by Alex Ayliffe

I wanted a dog,
a dog for my birthday.

To walk with,
to talk with,

to feed and to pat.

"Well, let's get a big dog,
a huge dog," Dad said,
"a gentle giant that knocks you flat!"

But Sue thought a big dog might frighten her cat.

Granny wanted a shaggy dog
to keep her feet warm.

And Mom thought the dog should be neat and clean.

"Hang on!" I said.
"This is supposed
to be my dog!
I know what I want,
you'll just have to wait
and see!"

But they argued nonstop
until we got to the shop,

then Lucy bounced forward

and she
chose me!